P9-CDW-170

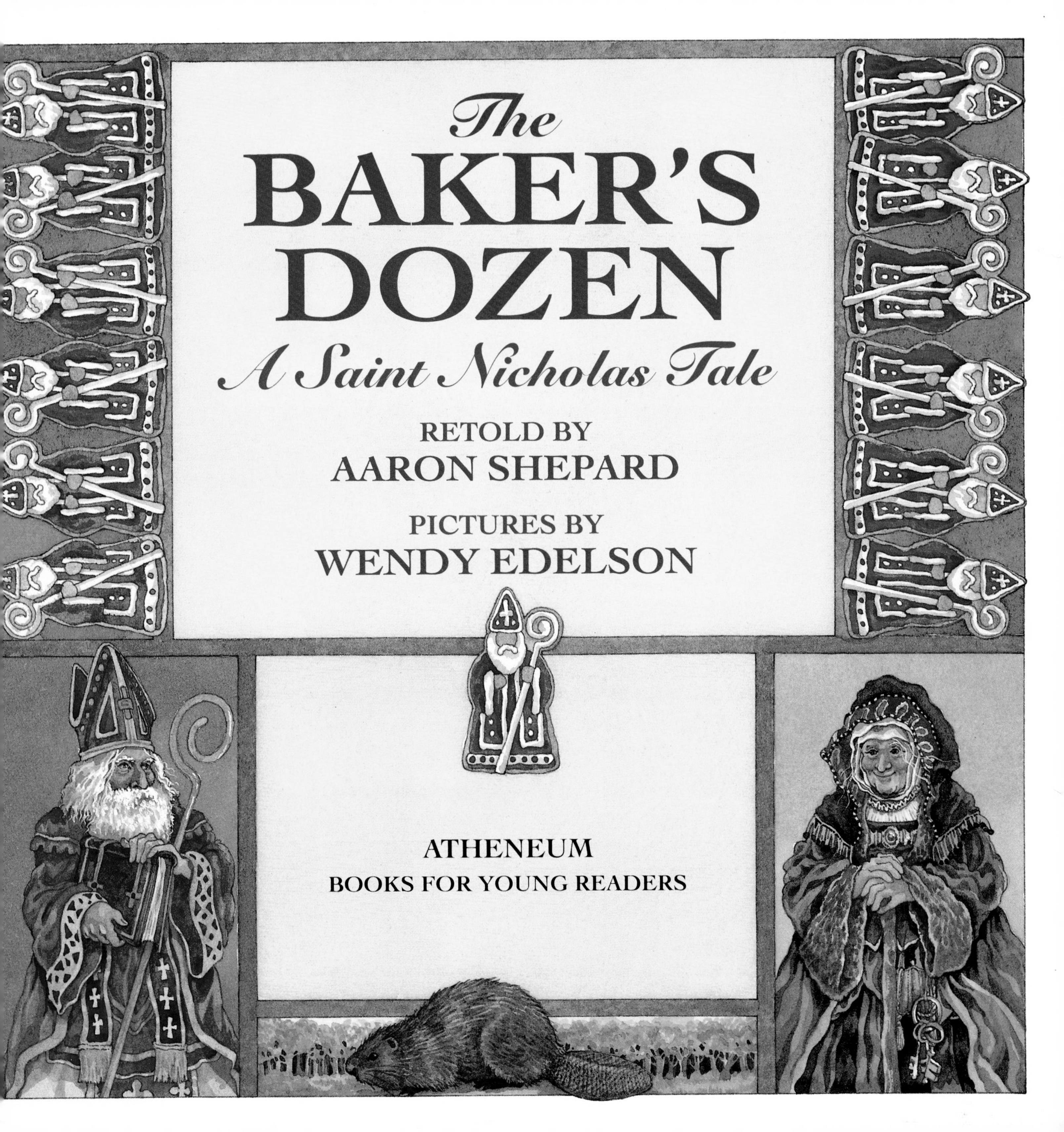

The BAKER'S DOZEN

A Saint Nicholas Tale

RETOLD BY
AARON SHEPARD

PICTURES BY
WENDY EDELSON

ATHENEUM
BOOKS FOR YOUNG READERS

For Clare Costello
—A.S.

For Cynthia and Zvi Edelson, with love
—W.E.

Though a number of sources were used for this retelling, the earliest and most authoritative was *Myths and Legends of Our Own Land,* by Charles M. Skinner, Lippincott, Philadelphia and London, 1896; reprinted by Singing Tree Press, Detroit, 1969. For inspiration and a crucial element, I am indebted to storyteller Sheila Dailey and her wonderful audio tape *Stories of the Long Christmas,* Rumpelstiltskin Productions, P. O. Box 2020, Mt. Pleasant, MI 48858, 1986.

Atheneum Books for Young Readers
An imprint of Simon & Schuster Children's Publishing Division
1230 Avenue of the Americas
New York, New York 10020

The text of this book is set in Cochin.
The illustrations were done in water color.

Printed in U.S.A.

First edition
10 9 8 7 6 5 4 3 2 1

Library of Congress Cataloging-in-Publication Data
Shepard, Aaron.
The baker's dozen : a St. Nicholas tale / Aaron Shepard : pictures by Wendy Edelson. — 1st ed. p. cm.
Summary: A legend of colonial America in which a greedy baker learns the importance of generosity in business, thus initiating the custom of the "baker's dozen."
ISBN 0-689-80298-6
[1. Folklore — United States.] I. Edelson, Wendy, ill. II. Title.
PZ8.1.S53945Bak 1995 398.21 — dc20 [E] 92 38261 CIP AC

The BAKER'S DOZEN

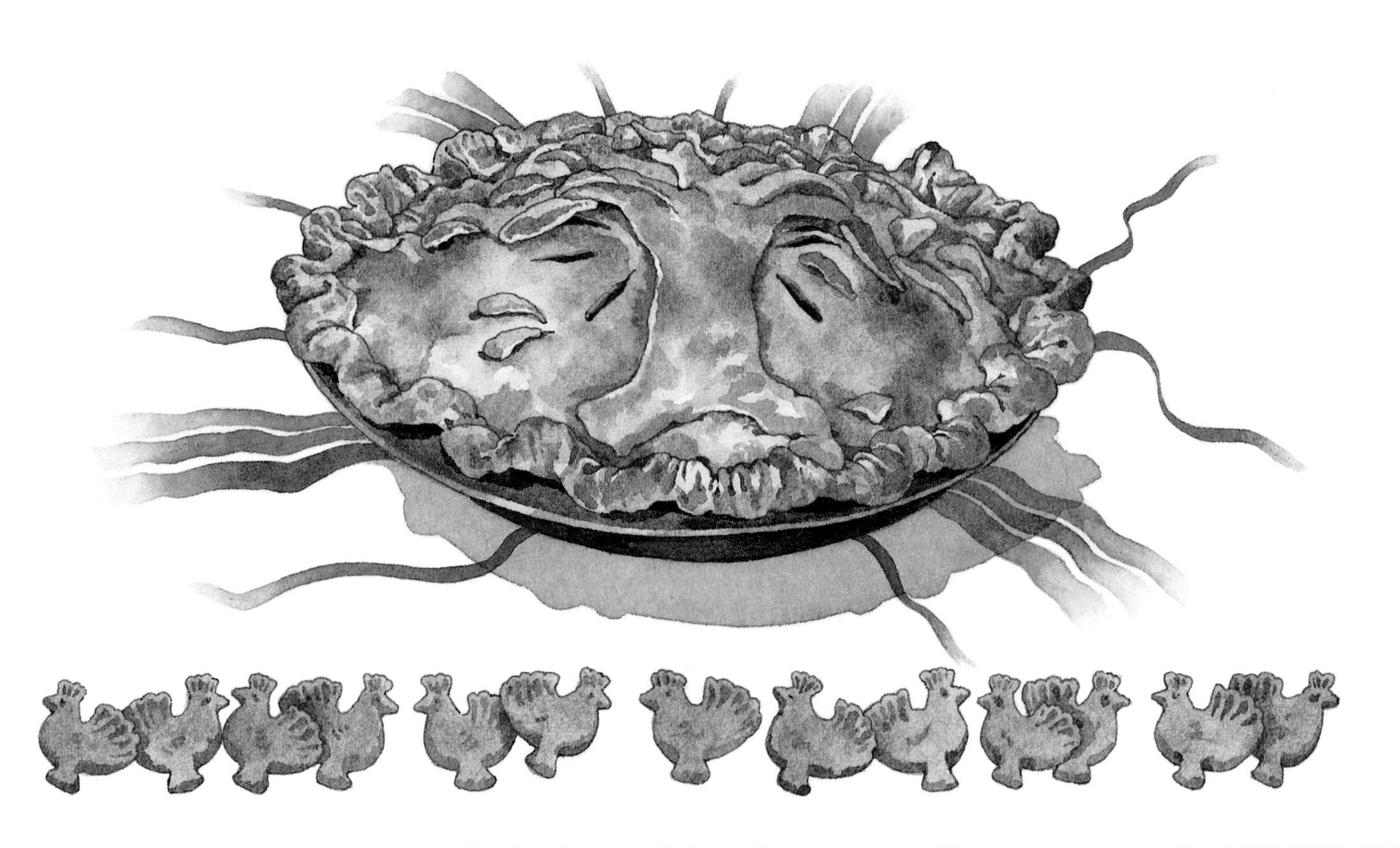

In the Dutch colonial town later known as Albany, New York,

there lived a baker, Van Amsterdam, who was as honest as he could be. Each morning he checked and balanced his scales, and he took great care to give his customers exactly what they paid for—not more and not less.

Van Amsterdam's shop was always busy, because people trusted him, and because he was a good baker as well. And never was the shop busier than in the days before December 6, when the Dutch celebrate Saint Nicholas Day.

At that time of year people flocked to the baker's shop to buy his fine Saint Nicholas cookies. Made of gingerbread, iced in red and white, they looked just like Saint Nicholas as the Dutch know him—tall and thin, with a high, red bishop's cap, and a long, red bishop's cloak.

One Saint Nicholas Day morning the baker was just ready for business, when the door of his shop flew open. In walked an old woman, wrapped in a long black shawl.

"I have come for a dozen of your Saint Nicholas cookies."

Taking a tray, Van Amsterdam counted out twelve cookies. He started to wrap them, but the woman reached out and stopped him.

"I asked for a dozen. You have given me only twelve."

"Madam," said the baker, "everyone knows that a dozen *is* twelve."

"But I say a dozen is thirteen," said the woman. "Give me one more."

Van Amsterdam was not a man to bear foolishness. "Madam, my customers get exactly what they pay for—not more and not less."

"Then you may keep the cookies," the woman said. She turned to go, but stopped at the door.

"Van Amsterdam! However honest you may be, your heart is small and your fist is tight. *Fall again, mount again, learn how to count again!*"

Then she was gone.

From that day everything went wrong in Van Amsterdam's bakery. His bread rose too high or not at all. His pies were sour or too sweet. His cakes crumbled or were chewy. His cookies were burnt or doughy.

His customers soon noticed the difference. Before long most of them were going to other bakers.

"That old woman has bewitched me," said the baker to himself. "Is this how my honesty is rewarded?"

A year passed. The baker grew poorer and poorer. Since he sold little, he baked little, and his shelves were nearly bare. His last few customers slipped away.

Finally, on the day before Saint Nicholas Day, not one customer came to Van Amsterdam's shop. At day's end the baker sat alone, staring at his unsold Saint Nicholas cookies.

"I wish Saint Nicholas could help me now," he said. Then he closed his shop and went sadly to bed.

That night, the baker had a dream. He was a boy again, one in a crowd of happy children. And there in the midst of them was Saint Nicholas himself.

The bishop's white horse stood beside him, its baskets filled with gifts. Nicholas pulled out one gift after another, and handed them to the children. But Van Amsterdam noticed something strange. No matter how many presents Nicholas passed out, there were always more to give. In fact the more he took from the baskets, the more they seemed to hold.

Then Nicholas handed a gift to Van Amsterdam. It was one of the baker's own Saint Nicholas cookies! Van Amsterdam looked up to thank him, but it was no longer Saint Nicholas standing there.

Smiling down at him was the old woman with the long black shawl.

Van Amsterdam awoke with a start. Moonlight shone through the cracks around the shutters as he lay there, thinking.

"I always give my customers exactly what they pay for," he said to himself, "not more and not less. But why *not* give more?"

The next morning, Saint Nicholas Day, the baker rose early. He mixed his gingerbread dough and rolled it out.

He cut the shapes and baked them. He iced them in red and white to look just like Saint Nicholas. And the cookies were as fine as any he had made.

Van Amsterdam had just finished, when the door flew open. In walked the old woman with the long black shawl.

"I have come for a dozen of your Saint Nicholas cookies."

In great excitement, Van Amsterdam counted out twelve cookies—and one more.

"In this shop," he said, "from now on, a dozen is thirteen."

"You have learned to count well," said the woman. "You will surely be rewarded."

She paid for the cookies and started out. But as the door swung shut, the baker's eyes seemed to play a trick on him. He thought he glimpsed the tail end of a long red cloak.

As the old woman foretold, Van Amsterdam *was* rewarded. When people heard he counted thirteen as a dozen, he had more customers than ever.

In fact Van Amsterdam grew so wealthy that the other bakers in town began doing the same. From there the practice spread to other towns, and at last through all the American colonies.

And this, they say, is how thirteen became the "baker's dozen"—a custom common for over a century—

and alive in some places to this day.